William Butler Yeats

Per Amica Silentia Lunae

Outlook

William Butler Yeats

Per Amica Silentia Lunae

1. Auflage | ISBN: 978-3-73261-854-5

Erscheinungsort: Paderborn, Deutschland

Erscheinungsjahr: 2018

Outlook Verlag GmbH, Paderborn.

William Butler Yeats

Per Amica Silentia Lunae

Outlook

PER AMICA SILENTIA LUNAE

PER AMICA SILENTIA LUNAE

SPECIAL LIMITED EDITION

PER AMICA
SILENTIA LUNAE

BY
WILLIAM BUTLER YEATS

New York
THE MACMILLAN COMPANY
1918
All rights reserved

Norwood Press
J. S. Cushing Co.—Berwick & SmithCo.
Norwood, Mass., U.S.A.

PROLOGUE

My Dear "Maurice"—You will remember that afternoon in Calvados last summer when your black Persian "Minoulooshe," who had walked behind us for a good mile, heard a wing flutter in a bramble-bush? For a long time we called her endearing names in vain. She seemed resolute to spend her night among the brambles. She had interrupted a conversation, often interrupted before, upon certain thoughts so long habitual that I may be permitted to call them my convictions. When I came back to London my mind ran again and again to those conversations and I could not rest till I had written out in this little book all that I had said or would have said. Read it some day when "Minoulooshe" is asleep.

W. B. YEATS.

May 11, 1917.

EGO DOMINUS TUUS

H_{IC}

On the grey sand beside the shallow stream,
Under your old wind-beaten tower, where still
A lamp burns on above the open book
That Michael Robartes left, you walk in the moon,
And, though you have passed the best of life, still trace,
Enthralled by the unconquerable delusion,
Magical shapes.

I_{LLE}

By the help of an image
I call to my own opposite, summon all
That I have handled least, least looked upon.

H_{IC}

And I would find myself and not an image.

I_{LLE}

That is our modern hope, and by its light
We have lit upon the gentle, sensitive mind
And lost the old nonchalance of the hand;
Whether we have chosen chisel, pen, or brush,
We are but critics, or but half create,
Timid, entangled, empty, and abashed,
Lacking the countenance of our friends.

H_{IC}

And yet,
The chief imagination of Christendom,
Dante Alighieri, so utterly found himself,
That he has made that hollow face of his
More plain to the mind's eye than any face
But that of Christ.

I_{LLE}

And did he find himself,
Or was the hunger that had made it hollow
A hunger for the apple on the bough
Most out of reach? And is that spectral image
The man that Lapo and that Guido knew?
I think he fashioned from his opposite
An image that might have been a stony face,
Staring upon a Beduin's horse-hair roof,
From doored and windowed cliff, or half upturned
Among the coarse grass and the camel dung.
He set his chisel to the hardest stone;
Being mocked by Guido for his lecherous life,
Derided and deriding, driven out
To climb that stair and eat that bitter bread,
He found the unpersuadable justice, he found
The most exalted lady loved by a man.

Hıc

Yet surely there are men who have made their art
Out of no tragic war; lovers of life,
Impulsive men, that look for happiness,
And sing when they have found it.

Iℓℓℇ

             No, not sing,
For those that love the world serve it in action,
Grow rich, popular, and full of influence;
And should they paint or write still is it action,
The struggle of the fly in marmalade.
The rhetorician would deceive his neighbours,
The sentimentalist himself; while art
Is but a vision of reality.
What portion in the world can the artist have,
Who has awakened from the common dream,
But dissipation and despair?

Hıc

             And yet,
No one denies to Keats love of the world,
Remember his deliberate happiness.

Ille

His art is happy, but who knows his mind?
I see a schoolboy, when I think of him,
With face and nose pressed to a sweetshop window,
For certainly he sank into his grave,
His senses and his heart unsatisfied;
And made—being poor, ailing and ignorant,
Shut out from all the luxury of the world,
The ill-bred son of a livery stable keeper—
Luxuriant song.

Hic

        Why should you leave the lamp
Burning alone beside an open book,
And trace these characters upon the sand?
A style is found by sedentary toil,
And by the imitation of great masters.

Ille

Because I seek an image, not a book;
Those men that in their writings are most wise
Own nothing but their blind, stupefied hearts.
I call to the mysterious one who yet
Shall walk the wet sand by the water's edge,
And look most like me, being indeed my double,
And prove of all imaginable things
The most unlike, being my anti-self,
And, standing by these characters, disclose
All that I seek; and whisper it as though
He were afraid the birds, who cry aloud
Their momentary cries before it is dawn,
Would carry it away to blasphemous men.

December 1915.

PER AMICA SILENTIA LUNAE

ANIMA HOMINIS

I

When I come home after meeting men who are strange to me, and sometimes even after talking to women, I go over all I have said in gloom and disappointment. Perhaps I have overstated everything from a desire to vex or startle, from hostility that is but fear; or all my natural thoughts have been drowned by an undisciplined sympathy. My fellow-diners have hardly seemed of mixed humanity, and how should I keep my head among images of good and evil, crude allegories.

But when I shut my door and light the candle, I invite a Marmorean Muse, an art, where no thought or emotion has come to mind because another man has thought or felt something different, for now there must be no reaction, action only, and the world must move my heart but to the heart's discovery of itself, and I begin to dream of eyelids that do not quiver before the bayonet: all my thoughts have ease and joy, I am all virtue and confidence. When I come to put in rhyme what I have found it will be a hard toil, but for a moment I believe I have found myself and not my anti-self. It is only the shrinking from toil perhaps that convinces me that I have been no more myself than is the cat the medicinal grass it is eating in the garden.

How could I have mistaken for myself an heroic condition that from early boyhood has made me superstitious? That which comes as complete, as minutely organised, as are those elaborate, brightly lighted buildings and sceneries appearing in a moment, as I lie between sleeping and waking, must come from above me and beyond me. At times I remember that place in Dante where he sees in his chamber the "Lord of Terrible Aspect," and how, seeming "to rejoice inwardly that it was a marvel to see, speaking, he said, many things among the which I could understand but few, and of these this: ego dominus tuus"; or should the conditions come, not as it were in a gesture
—as the image of a man—but in some fine landscape, it is of Boehme, maybe, that I think, and of that country where we "eternally solace ourselves in the excellent beautiful flourishing of all manner of flowers and forms, both trees and plants, and all kinds of fruit."

II

When I consider the minds of my friends, among artists and emotional writers, I discover a like contrast. I have sometimes told one close friend that her only fault is a habit of harsh judgment with those who have not her sympathy, and she has written comedies where the wickedest people seem but bold children. She does not know why she has created that world where no one is ever judged, a high celebration of indulgence, but to me it seems that her ideal of beauty is the compensating dream of a nature wearied out by over-much judgment. I know a famous actress who in private life is like the captain of some buccaneer ship holding his crew to good behaviour at the mouth of a blunderbuss, and upon the stage she excels in the representation of women who stir to pity and to desire because they need our protection, and is most adorable as one of those young queens imagined by Maeterlinck who have so little will, so little self, that they are like shadows sighing at the edge of the world. When I last saw her in her own house she lived in a torrent of words and movements, she could not listen, and all about her upon the walls were women drawn by Burne-Jones in his latest period. She had invited me in the hope that I would defend those women, who were always listening, and are as necessary to her as a contemplative Buddha to a Japanese Samurai, against a French critic who would persuade her to take into her heart in their stead a Post-Impressionist picture of a fat, ruddy, nude woman lying upon a Turkey carpet.

There are indeed certain men whose art is less an opposing virtue than a compensation for some accident of health or circumstance. During the riots over the first production of the *Playboy of the Western World* Synge was confused, without clear thought, and was soon ill—indeed the strain of that week may perhaps have hastened his death—and he was, as is usual with gentle and silent men, scrupulously accurate in all his statements. In his art he made, to delight his ear and his mind's eye, voluble daredevils who "go romancing through a romping lifetime ... to the dawning of the Judgment Day." At other moments this man, condemned to the life of a monk by bad health, takes an amused pleasure in "great queens ... making themselves matches from the start to the end." Indeed, in all his imagination he delights in fine physical life, in life where the moon pulls up the tide. The last act of *Deirdre of the Sorrows*, where his art is at its noblest, was written upon his death-bed. He was not sure of any world to come, he was leaving his betrothed and his unwritten play—"Oh, what a waste of time," he said to me; he hated to die, and in the last speeches of Deirdre and in the middle act he accepted death and dismissed life with a gracious gesture. He gave to Deirdre the emotion that seemed to him most desirable, most difficult, most fitting, and maybe saw in those delighted seven years, now dwindling from her, the fulfilment of his own life.

III

When I think of any great poetical writer of the past (a realist is an historian and obscures the cleavage by the record of his eyes) I comprehend, if I know the lineaments of his life, that the work is the man's flight from his entire horoscope, his blind struggle in the network of the stars. William Morris, a happy, busy, most irascible man, described dim colour and pensive emotion, following, beyond any man of his time, an indolent muse; while Savage Landor topped us all in calm nobility when the pen was in his hand, as in the daily violence of his passion when he had laid it down. He had in his *Imaginary Conversations* reminded us, as it were, that the Venus de Milo is a stone, and yet he wrote when the copies did not come from the printer as soon as he expected: "I have ... had the resolution to tear in pieces all my sketches and projects and to forswear all future undertakings. I have tried to sleep away my time and pass two-thirds of the twenty-four hours in bed. I may speak of myself as a dead man." I imagine Keats to have been born with that thirst for luxury common to many at the outsetting of the Romantic Movement, and not able, like wealthy Beckford, to slake it with beautiful and strange objects. It drove him to imaginary delights; ignorant, poor, and in poor health, and not perfectly well-bred, he knew himself driven from tangible luxury; meeting Shelley, he was resentful and suspicious because he, as Leigh Hunt recalls, "being a little too sensitive on the score of his origin, felt inclined to see in every man of birth his natural enemy."

IV

Some thirty years ago I read a prose allegory by Simeon Solomon, long out of print and unprocurable, and remember or seem to remember a sentence, "a hollow image of fulfilled desire." All happy art seems to me that hollow image, but when its lineaments express also the poverty or the exasperation that set its maker to the work, we call it tragic art. Keats but gave us his dream of luxury; but while reading Dante we never long escape the conflict, partly because the verses are at moments a mirror of his history, and yet more because that history is so clear and simple that it has the quality of art. I am no Dante scholar, and I but read him in Shadwell or in Dante Rossetti, but I am always persuaded that he celebrated the most pure lady poet ever sung and the Divine Justice, not merely because death took that lady and Florence banished her singer, but because he had to struggle in his own heart with his unjust anger and his lust; while unlike those of the great poets, who are at peace with the world and at war with themselves, he fought a double war. "Always," says Boccaccio, "both in youth and maturity he found room among his virtues for lechery"; or as Matthew Arnold preferred to change the phrase, "his conduct was exceeding irregular." Guido Cavalcanti, as Rossetti translates him, finds "too much baseness" in his friend:

> "And still thy speech of me, heartfelt and kind,
> Hath made me treasure up thy poetry;
> But now I dare not, for thy abject life,
> Make manifest that I approve thy rhymes."

And when Dante meets Beatrice in Eden, does she not reproach him because, when she had taken her presence away, he followed in spite of warning dreams, false images, and now, to save him in his own despite, she has "visited ... the Portals of the Dead," and chosen Virgil for his courier? While Gino da Pistoia complains that in his *Commedia* his "lovely heresies ... beat the right down and let the wrong go free":

> "Therefore his vain decrees, wherein he lied,
> Must be like empty nutshells flung aside;
> Yet through the rash false witness set to grow,
> French and Italian vengeance on such pride
> May fall like Anthony on Cicero."

Dante himself sings to Giovanni Guirino "at the approach of death";

> "The King, by whose rich grave his servants be
> With plenty beyond measure set to dwell,
> Ordains that I my bitter wrath dispel,
> And lift mine eyes to the great Consistory."

V

We make out of the quarrel with others, rhetoric, but of the quarrel with ourselves, poetry. Unlike the rhetoricians, who get a confident voice from remembering the crowd they have won or may win, we sing amid our uncertainty; and, smitten even in the presence of the most high beauty by the knowledge of our solitude, our rhythm shudders. I think, too, that no fine poet, no matter how disordered his life, has ever, even in his mere life, had pleasure for his end. Johnson and Dowson, friends of my youth, were dissipated men, the one a drunkard, the other a drunkard and mad about women, and yet they had the gravity of men who had found life out and were awakening from the dream; and both, one in life and art and one in art and less in life, had a continual preoccupation with religion. Nor has any poet I have read of or heard of or met with been a sentimentalist. The other self, the anti-self or the antithetical self, as one may choose to name it, comes but to those who are no longer deceived, whose passion is reality. The sentimentalists are practical men who believe in money, in position, in a marriage bell, and whose understanding of happiness is to be so busy whether at work or at play, that all is forgotten but the momentary aim. They find their pleasure in a cup that is filled from Lethe's wharf, and for the awakening, for the vision, for the revelation of reality, tradition offers us a different word— ecstasy. An old artist wrote to me of his wanderings by the quays of New York, and how he found there a woman nursing a sick child, and drew her story from her. She spoke, too, of other children who had died: a long tragic story. "I wanted to paint her," he wrote, "if I denied myself any of the pain I could not believe in my own ecstasy." We must not make a false faith by hiding from our thoughts the causes of doubt, for faith is the highest achievement of the human intellect, the only gift man can make to God, and therefore it must be offered in sincerity. Neither must we create, by hiding ugliness, a false beauty as our offering to the world. He only can create the greatest imaginable beauty who has endured all imaginable pangs, for only when we have seen and foreseen what we dread shall we be rewarded by that dazzling unforeseen wing-footed wanderer. We could not find him if he were not in some sense of our being and yet of our being but as water with fire, a noise with silence. He is of all things not impossible the most difficult, for that only which comes easily can never be a portion of our being, "Soon got, soon gone," as the proverb says. I shall find the dark grow luminous, the void fruitful when I understand I have nothing, that the ringers in the tower have appointed for the hymen of the soul a passing bell.

The last knowledge has often come most quickly to turbulent men, and for a season brought new turbulence. When life puts away her conjuring tricks one by one, those that deceive us longest may well be the wine-cup and the sensual kiss, for our Chambers of Commerce and of Commons have not the divine architecture of the body, nor has their frenzy been ripened by the sun. The poet, because he may not stand within the sacred house but lives amid the whirlwinds that beset its threshold, may find his pardon.

VI

I think the Christian saint and hero, instead of being merely dissatisfied, make deliberate sacrifice. I remember reading once an autobiography of a man who had made a daring journey in disguise to Russian exiles in Siberia, and his telling how, very timid as a child, he schooled himself by wandering at night through dangerous streets. Saint and hero cannot be content to pass at moments to that hollow image and after become their heterogeneous selves, but would always, if they could, resemble the antithetical self. There is a shadow of type on type, for in all great poetical styles there is saint or hero, but when it is all over Dante can return to his chambering and Shakespeare to his "pottle pot." They sought no impossible perfection but when they handled paper or parchment. So too will saint or hero, because he works in his own flesh and blood and not in paper or parchment, have more deliberate understanding of that other flesh and blood.

Some years ago I began to believe that our culture, with its doctrine of sincerity and self-realisation, made us gentle and passive, and that the Middle Ages and the Renaissance were right to found theirs upon the imitation of Christ or of some classic hero. St. Francis and Caesar Borgia made themselves over-mastering, creative persons by turning from the mirror to meditation upon a mask. When I had this thought I could see nothing else in life. I could not write the play I had planned, for all became allegorical, and though I tore up hundreds of pages in my endeavour to escape from allegory, my imagination became sterile for nearly five years and I only escaped at last when I had mocked in a comedy my own thought. I was always thinking of the element of imitation in style and in life, and of the life beyond heroic imitation. I find in an old diary: "I think all happiness depends on the energy to assume the mask of some other life, on a re-birth as something not one's self, something created in a moment and perpetually renewed; in playing a game like that of a child where one loses the infinite pain of self-realisation, in a grotesque or solemn painted face put on that one may hide from the terror of judgment.... Perhaps all the sins and energies of the world are but the world's flight from an infinite blinding beam"; and again at an earlier date: "If we cannot imagine ourselves as different from what we are, and try to assume that second self, we cannot impose a discipline upon ourselves though we may accept one from others. Active virtue, as distinguished from the passive acceptance of a code, is therefore theatrical, consciously dramatic, the wearing of a mask.... Wordsworth, great poet though he be, is so often flat and heavy partly because his moral sense, being a discipline he had not created, a mere obedience, has no theatrical element. This increases his popularity with the better kind of journalists and politicians who have written books."

VII

I thought the hero found hanging upon some oak of Dodona an ancient mask, where perhaps there lingered something of Egypt, and that he changed it to his fancy, touching it a little here and there, gilding the eyebrows or putting a gilt line where the cheekbone comes; that when at last he looked out of its eyes he knew another's breath came and went within his breath upon the carven lips, and that his eyes were upon the instant fixed upon a visionary world: how else could the god have come to us in the forest? The good, unlearned books say that He who keeps the distant stars within His fold comes without intermediary, but Plutarch's precepts and the experience of old women in Soho, ministering their witchcraft to servant girls at a shilling apiece, will have it that a strange living man may win for Daemon an illustrious dead man; but now I add another thought: the Daemon comes not as like to like but seeking its own opposite, for man and Daemon feed the hunger in one another's hearts. Because the ghost is simple, the man heterogeneous and confused, they are but knit together when the man has found a mask whose lineaments permit the expression of all the man most lacks, and it may be dreads, and of that only.

The more insatiable in all desire, the more resolute to refuse deception or an easy victory, the more close will be the bond, the more violent and definite the antipathy.

VIII

I think that all religious men have believed that there is a hand not ours in the events of life, and that, as somebody says in *Wilhelm Meister*, accident is destiny; and I think it was Heraclitus who said: the Daemon is our destiny. When I think of life as a struggle with the Daemon who would ever set us to the hardest work among those not impossible, I understand why there is a deep enmity between a man and his destiny, and why a man loves nothing but his destiny. In an Anglo-Saxon poem a certain man is called, as though to call him something that summed up all heroism, "Doom eager." I am persuaded that the Daemon delivers and deceives us, and that he wove that netting from the stars and threw the net from his shoulder. Then my imagination runs from Daemon to sweetheart, and I divine an analogy that evades the intellect. I remember that Greek antiquity has bid us look for the principal stars, that govern enemy and sweetheart alike, among those that are about to set, in the Seventh House as the astrologers say; and that it may be "sexual love," which is "founded upon spiritual hate," is an image of the warfare of man and Daemon; and I even wonder if there may not be some secret communion, some whispering in the dark between Daemon and sweetheart. I remember how often women, when in love, grow superstitious, and believe that they can bring their lovers good luck; and I remember an old Irish story of three young men who went seeking for help in battle into the house of the gods at Slieve-na-mon. "You must first be married," some god told them, "because a man's good or evil luck comes to him through a woman."

I sometimes fence for half-an-hour at the day's end, and when I close my eyes upon the pillow I see a foil playing before me, the button to my face. We meet always in the deep of the mind, whatever our work, wherever our reverie carries us, that other Will.

IX

The poet finds and makes his mask in disappointment, the hero in defeat. The desire that is satisfied is not a great desire, nor has the shoulder used all its might that an unbreakable gate has never strained. The saint alone is not deceived, neither thrusting with his shoulder nor holding out unsatisfied hands. He would climb without wandering to the antithetical self of the world, the Indian narrowing his thought in meditation or driving it away in contemplation, the Christian copying Christ, the antithetical self of the classic world. For a hero loves the world till it breaks him, and the poet till it has broken faith; but while the world was yet debonair, the saint has turned away, and because he renounced Experience itself, he will wear his mask as he finds it. The poet or the hero, no matter upon what bark they found their mask, so teeming their fancy, somewhat change its lineaments, but the saint, whose life is but a round of customary duty, needs nothing the whole world does not need, and day by day he scourges in his body the Roman and Christian conquerors: Alexander and Caesar are famished in his cell. His nativity is neither in disappointment nor in defeat, but in a temptation like that of Christ in the Wilderness, a contemplation in a single instant perpetually renewed of the Kingdom of the World; all, because all renounced, continually present showing their empty thrones. Edwin Ellis, remembering that Christ also measured the sacrifice, imagined himself in a fine poem as meeting at Golgotha the phantom of "Christ the Less," the Christ who might have lived a prosperous life without the knowledge of sin, and who now wanders "companionless a weary spectre day and night."

> "I saw him go and cried to him
> 'Eli, thou hast forsaken me.'
> The nails were burning through each limb,
> He fled to find felicity."

And yet is the saint spared, despite his martyr's crown and his vigil of desire, defeat, disappointed love, and the sorrow of parting.

> "O Night, that did'st lead thus,
> O Night, more lovely than the dawn of light,
> O Night, that broughtest us
> Lover to lover's sight,
> Lover with loved in marriage of delight!
>
> Upon my flowery breast,
> Wholly for him, and save himself for none,
> There did I give sweet rest
> To my beloved one;
> The fanning of the cedars breathed thereon.
>
> When the first morning air
> Blew from the tower, and waved his locks aside,
> His hand, with gentle care,
> Did wound me in the side,
> And in my body all my senses died.
>
> All things I then forgot,
> My cheek on him who for my coming came;
> All ceased and I was not,
> Leaving my cares and shame
> Among the lilies, and forgetting them."[1]

X

It is not permitted to a man, who takes up pen or chisel, to seek originality, for passion is his only business, and he cannot but mould or sing after a new fashion because no disaster is like another. He is like those phantom lovers in the Japanese play who, compelled to wander side by side and never mingle, cry: "We neither wake nor sleep and passing our nights in a sorrow which is in the end a vision, what are these scenes of spring to us?" If when we have found a mask we fancy that it will not match our mood till we have touched with gold the cheek, we do it furtively, and only where the oaks of Dodona cast their deepest shadow, for could he see our handiwork the Daemon would fling himself out, being our enemy.

XI

Many years ago I saw, between sleeping and waking, a woman of incredible beauty shooting an arrow into the sky, and from the moment when I made my first guess at her meaning I have thought much of the difference between the winding movement of nature and the straight line, which is called in Balzac's *Seraphita* the "Mark of Man," but comes closer to my meaning as the mark of saint or sage. I think that we who are poets and artists, not being permitted to shoot beyond the tangible, must go from desire to weariness and so to desire again, and live but for the moment when vision comes to our weariness like terrible lightning, in the humility of the brutes. I do not doubt those heaving circles, those winding arcs, whether in one man's life or in that of an age, are mathematical, and that some in the world, or beyond the world, have foreknown the event and pricked upon the calendar the life-span of a Christ, a Buddha, a Napoleon: that every movement, in feeling or in thought, prepares in the dark by its own increasing clarity and confidence its own executioner. We seek reality with the slow toil of our weakness and are smitten from the boundless and the unforeseen. Only when we are saint or sage, and renounce Experience itself, can we, in the language of the Christian Caballa, leave the sudden lightning and the path of the serpent and become the bowman who aims his arrow at the centre of the sun.

XII

The doctors of medicine have discovered that certain dreams of the night, for I do not grant them all, are the day's unfulfilled desire, and that our terror of desires condemned by the conscience has distorted and disturbed our dreams. They have only studied the breaking into dream of elements that have remained unsatisfied without purifying discouragement. We can satisfy in life a few of our passions and each passion but a little, and our characters indeed but differ because no two men bargain alike. The bargain, the compromise, is always threatened, and when it is broken we become mad or hysterical or are in some way deluded; and so when a starved or banished passion shows in a dream we, before awaking, break the logic that had given it the capacity of action and throw it into chaos again. But the passions, when we know that they cannot find fulfilment, become vision; and a vision, whether we wake or sleep, prolongs its power by rhythm and pattern, the wheel where the world is butterfly. We need no protection, but it does, for if we become interested in ourselves, in our own lives, we pass out of the vision. Whether it is we or the vision that create the pattern, who set the wheel turning, it is hard to say, but certainly we have a hundred ways of keeping it near us: we select our images from past times, we turn from our own age and try to feel Chaucer nearer than the daily paper. It compels us to cover all it cannot incorporate, and would carry us when it comes in sleep to that moment when even sleep closes her eyes and dreams begin to dream; and we are taken up into a clear light and are forgetful even of our own names and actions and yet in perfect possession of ourselves murmur like Faust, "Stay, moment," and murmur in vain.

XIII

A poet, when he is growing old, will ask himself if he cannot keep his mask and his vision without new bitterness, new disappointment. Could he if he would, knowing how frail his vigour from youth up, copy Landor who lived loving and hating, ridiculous and unconquered, into extreme old age, all lost but the favour of his muses.

> The mother of the muses we are taught
> Is memory; she has left me; they remain
> And shake my shoulder urging me to sing.

Surely, he may think, now that I have found vision and mask I need not suffer any longer. He will buy perhaps some small old house where like Ariosto he can dig his garden, and think that in the return of birds and leaves, or moon and sun, and in the evening flight of the rooks he may discover rhythm and pattern like those in sleep and so never awake out of vision. Then he will remember Wordsworth withering into eighty years, honoured and empty-witted, and climb to some waste room and find, forgotten there by youth, some bitter crust.

February 25, 1917.

ANIMA MUNDI

I

I have always sought to bring my mind close to the mind of Indian and Japanese poets, old women in Connaught, mediums in Soho, lay brothers whom I imagine dreaming in some mediaeval monastery the dreams of their village, learned authors who refer all to antiquity; to immerse it in the general mind where that mind is scarce separable from what we have begun to call "the subconscious"; to liberate it from all that comes of councils and committees, from the world as it is seen from universities or from populous towns; and that I might so believe I have murmured evocations and frequented mediums, delighted in all that displayed great problems through sensuous images, or exciting phrases, accepting from abstract schools but a few technical words that are so old they seem but broken architraves fallen amid bramble and grass, and have put myself to school where all things are seen: *A Tenedo Tacitae per Amica Silentia Lunae*. At one time I thought to prove my conclusions by quoting from diaries where I have recorded certain strange events the moment they happened, but now I have changed my mind
—I will but say like the Arab boy that became Vizier: "O brother, I have taken stock in the desert sand and of the sayings of antiquity."

II

There is a letter of Goethe's, though I cannot remember where, that explains evocation, though he was but thinking of literature. He described some friend who had complained of literary sterility as too intelligent. One must allow the images to form with all their associations before one criticises. "If one is critical too soon," he wrote, "they will not form at all." If you suspend the critical faculty, I have discovered, either as the result of training, or, if you have the gift, by passing into a slight trance, images pass rapidly before you. If you can suspend also desire, and let them form at their own will, your absorption becomes more complete and they are more clear in colour, more precise in articulation, and you and they begin to move in the midst of what seems a powerful light. But the images pass before you linked by certain associations, and indeed in the first instance you have called them up by their association with traditional forms and sounds. You have discovered how, if you can but suspend will and intellect, to bring up from the "subconscious" anything you already possess a fragment of. Those who follow the old rule keep their bodies still and their minds awake and clear, dreading especially any confusion between the images of the mind and the objects of sense; they seek to become, as it were, polished mirrors.

I had no natural gift for this clear quiet, as I soon discovered, for my mind is abnormally restless; and I was seldom delighted by that sudden luminous definition of form which makes one understand almost in spite of oneself that one is not merely imagining. I therefore invented a new process. I had found that after evocation my sleep became at moments full of light and form, all that I had failed to find while awake; and I elaborated a symbolism of natural objects that I might give myself dreams during sleep, or rather visions, for they had none of the confusion of dreams, by laying upon my pillow or beside my bed certain flowers or leaves. Even to-day, after twenty years, the exaltations and the messages that came to me from bits of hawthorn or some other plant seem of all moments of my life the happiest and the wisest. After a time, perhaps because the novelty wearing off the symbol lost its power, or because my work at the Irish Theatre became too exciting, my sleep lost its responsiveness. I had fellow-scholars, and now it was I and now they who made some discovery. Before the mind's eye, whether in sleep or waking, came images that one was to discover presently in some book one had never read, and after looking in vain for explanation to the current theory of forgotten personal memory, I came to believe in a great memory passing on from generation to generation. But that was not enough, for these images showed intention and choice. They had a relation to what one knew and yet were an extension of one's knowledge. If no mind was there, why should I suddenly come upon salt and antimony, upon the liquefaction of the gold, as they were understood by the alchemists, or upon some detail of cabalistic symbolism verified at last by a learned scholar from his never-published manuscripts, and who can have put together so ingeniously, working by some law of association and yet with clear intention and personal application, certain mythological images. They had shown themselves to several minds, a fragment at a time, and had only shown their meaning when the puzzle picture had been put together. The thought was again and again before me that this study had created a contact or mingling with minds who had followed a like study in some other age, and that these minds still saw and thought and chose. Our daily thought was certainly but the line of foam at the shallow edge of a vast luminous sea: Henry More's *Anima Mundi*, Wordsworth's "immortal sea which brought us hither … and near whose edge the children sport," and in that sea there were some who swam or sailed, explorers who perhaps knew all its shores.

III

I had always to compel myself to fix the imagination upon the minds behind the personifications, and yet the personifications were themselves living and vivid. The minds that swayed these seemingly fluid images had doubtless form, and those images themselves seemed, as it were, mirrored in a living substance whose form is but change of form. From tradition and perception, one thought of one's own life as symbolised by earth, the place of heterogeneous things, the images as mirrored in water and the images themselves one could divine but as air; and beyond it all there was, I felt confident, certain aims and governing loves, the fire that makes all simple. Yet the images themselves were fourfold, and one judged their meaning in part from the predominance of one out of the four elements, or that of the fifth element, the veil hiding another four, a bird born out of the fire.

IV

I longed to know something even if it were but the family and Christian names of those minds that I could divine, and that yet remained always as it seemed impersonal. The sense of contact came perhaps but two or three times with clearness and certainty, but it left among all to whom it came some trace, a sudden silence, as it were, in the midst of thought or perhaps at moments of crisis a faint voice. Were our masters right when they declared so solidly that we should be content to know these presences that seemed friendly and near but as "the phantom" in Coleridge's poem, and to think of them perhaps, as having, as St. Thomas says, entered upon the eternal possession of themselves in one single moment?

> "All look and likeness caught from earth,
> All accident of kin and birth,
> Had passed away. There was no trace
> Of ought on that illumined face,
> Upraised beneath the rifted stone,
> But of one spirit all her own;
> She, she herself and only she,
> Shone through her body visibly."

V

One night I heard a voice that said: "The love of God for every human soul is infinite, for every human soul is unique; no other can satisfy the same need in God." Our masters had not denied that personality outlives the body or even that its rougher shape may cling to us a while after death, but only that we should seek it in those who are dead. Yet when I went among the country people, I found that they sought and found the old fragilities, infirmities, physiognomies that living stirred affection. The Spiddal knowledgeable man, who had his knowledge from his sister's ghost, noticed every hallowe'en, when he met her at the end of the garden, that her hair was greyer. Had she perhaps to exhaust her allotted years in the neighbourhood of her home, having died before her time? Because no authority seemed greater than that of this knowledge running backward to the beginning of the world, I began that study of spiritism so despised by Stanislas de Gaeta, the one eloquent learned scholar who has written of magic in our generation.

VI

I know much that I could never have known had I not learnt to consider in the after life what, there as here, is rough and disjointed; nor have I found that the mediums in Connaught and Soho have anything I cannot find some light on in Henry More, who was called during his life the holiest man now walking upon the earth.

All souls have a vehicle or body, and when one has said that, with More and the Platonists one has escaped from the abstract schools who seek always the power of some church or institution, and found oneself with great poetry, and superstition which is but popular poetry, in a pleasant dangerous world. Beauty is indeed but bodily life in some ideal condition. The vehicle of the human soul is what used to be called the animal spirits, and Henry More quotes from Hippocrates this sentence: "The mind of man is ... not nourished from meats and drinks from the belly, but by a clear luminous substance that redounds by separation from the blood." These animal spirits fill up all parts of the body and make up the body of air, as certain writers of the seventeenth century have called it. The soul has a plastic power, and can after death, or during life, should the vehicle leave the body for a while, mould it to any shape it will by an act of imagination, though the more unlike to the habitual that shape is, the greater the effort. To living and dead alike, the purity and abundance of the animal spirits are a chief power. The soul can mould from these an apparition clothed as if in life, and make it visible by showing it to our mind's eye, or by building into its substance certain particles drawn from the body of a medium till it is as visible and tangible as any other object. To help that building the ancients offered fragrant gum, the odour of flowers, and it may be pieces of virgin wax. The half materialised vehicle slowly exudes from the skin in dull luminous drops or condenses from a luminous cloud, the light fading as weight and density increase. The witch, going beyond the medium, offered to the slowly animating phantom certain drops of her blood. The vehicle once separate from the living man or woman may be moulded by the souls of others as readily as by its own soul, and even it seems by the souls of the living. It becomes a part for a while of that stream of images which I have compared to reflections upon water. But how does it follow that souls who never have handled the modelling tool or the brush, make perfect images? Those materialisations who imprint their powerful faces upon paraffin wax, leave there sculpture that would have taken a good artist, making and imagining, many hours. How did it follow that an ignorant woman could, as Henry More believed, project her vehicle in so good a likeness of a hare, that horse and hound and huntsman followed with the bugle blowing? Is not the problem the same as of those finely articulated scenes and patterns that come out of the dark, seemingly completed in the winking of an eye, as we are lying half asleep, and of all those elaborate images that drift in moments of inspiration or evocation before the mind's eye? Our animal spirits or vehicles are but as it were a condensation of the vehicle of *Anima Mundi*, and give substance to its images in the faint materialisation of our common thought, or more grossly when a ghost is our visitor. It should be no great feat, once those images have dipped into our vehicle, to take their portraits in the photographic camera. Henry More will have it that a hen scared by a hawk when the cock is treading, hatches out a hawkheaded chicken (I am no stickler for the fact), because before the soul of the unborn bird could give the shape "the deeply impassioned fancy of the mother" called from the general cistern of form a competing image. "The soul of the world," he runs on, "interposes and insinuates into all generations of things while the matter is fluid and yielding, which would induce a man to believe that she may not stand idle in the transformation of the vehicle of the daemons, but assist the fancies and desires, and so help to clothe them and to utter them according to their own pleasures; or it may be sometimes against their wills as the unwieldiness of the mother's fancy forces upon her a monstrous birth." Though images appear to flow and drift, it may be that we but change in our relation to them, now losing, now finding with the shifting of our minds; and certainly Henry More speaks by the book, claiming that those images may be hard to the right touch as "pillars of crystal" and as solidly coloured as our own to the right eyes. Shelley, a good Platonist, seems in his earliest work to set this general soul in the place of God, an opinion, one may find from More's friend Cudworth now affirmed, now combated, by classic authority; but More would steady us with a definition. The general soul as apart from its vehicle is "a substance incorporeal but without sense and animadversion pervading the whole matter of the universe and exercising a plastic power therein, according to the sundry predispositions and occasions, in the parts it works upon, raising such phenomena in the world, by directing the parts of the matter and their motion as cannot be resolved into mere mechanical powers." I must assume that "sense and animadversion," perception and direction, are always faculties of individual soul, and that, as Blake said, "God only acts or is in existing beings or men."

VII

The old theological conception of the individual soul as bodiless or abstract led to what Henry More calls "contradictory debate" as to how many angels "could dance booted and spurred upon the point of a needle," and made it possible for rationalist physiology to persuade us that our thought has no corporeal existence but in the molecules of the brain. Shelley was of opinion that the "thoughts which are called real or external objects" differed but in regularity of occurrence from "hallucinations, dreams and ideas of madmen," and noticed that he had dreamed, therefore lessening the difference, "three several times between intervals of two or more years the same precise dream." If all our mental images no less than apparitions (and I see no reason to distinguish) are forms existing in the general vehicle of *Anima Mundi*, and mirrored in our particular vehicle, many crooked things are made straight. I am persuaded that a logical process, or a series of related images, has body and period, and I think of *Anima Mundi* as a great pool or garden where it spreads through allotted growth like a great water plant or branches more fragrantly in the air. Indeed as Spenser's Garden of Adonis:

> "There is the first seminary
> Of all things that are born to live and die
> According to their kynds."

The soul by changes of "vital congruity," More says, draws to it a certain thought, and this thought draws by its association the sequence of many thoughts, endowing them with a life in the vehicle meted out according to the intensity of the first perception. A seed is set growing, and this growth may go on apart from the power, apart even from the knowledge of the soul. If I wish to "transfer" a thought I may think, let us say, of Cinderella's slipper, and my subject may see an old woman coming out of a chimney; or going to sleep I may wish to wake at seven o'clock and, though I never think of it again, I shall wake upon the instant. The thought has completed itself, certain acts of logic, turns, and knots in the stem have been accomplished out of sight and out of reach as it were. We are always starting these parasitic vegetables and letting them coil beyond our knowledge, and may become, like that lady in Balzac who, after a life of sanctity, plans upon her deathbed to fly with her renounced lover. After death a dream, a desire she had perhaps ceased to believe in, perhaps ceased almost to remember, must have recurred again and again with its anguish and its happiness. We can only refuse to start the wandering sequence or, if start it does, hold it in the intellectual light where time gallops, and so keep it from slipping down into the sluggish vehicle. The toil of the living is to free themselves from an endless sequence of objects, and that of the dead to free themselves from an endless sequence of thoughts. One sequence begets another, and these have power because of all those things we do, not for their own sake but for an imagined good.

VIII

Spiritism, whether of folk-lore or of the séance room, the visions of Swedenborg, and the speculation of the Platonists and Japanese plays, will have it that we may see at certain roads and in certain houses old murders acted over again, and in certain fields dead huntsmen riding with horse and hound, or ancient armies fighting above bones or ashes. We carry to *Anima Mundi* our memory, and that memory is for a time our external world; and all passionate moments recur again and again, for passion desires its own recurrence more than any event, and whatever there is of corresponding complacency or remorse is our beginning of judgment; nor do we remember only the events of life, for thoughts bred of longing and of fear, all those parasitic vegetables that have slipped through our fingers, come again like a rope's end to smite us upon the face; and as Cornelius Agrippa writes: "We may dream ourselves to be consumed in flame and persecuted by daemons," and certain spirits have complained that they would be hard put to it to arouse those who died, believing they could not awake till a trumpet shrilled. A ghost in a Japanese play is set afire by a fantastic scruple, and though a Buddhist priest explains that the fire would go out of itself if the ghost but ceased to believe in it, it cannot cease to believe. Cornelius Agrippa called such dreaming souls hobgoblins, and when Hamlet refused the bare bodkin because of what dreams may come, it was from no mere literary fancy. The soul can indeed, it appears, change these objects built about us by the memory, as it may change its shape; but the greater the change, the greater the effort and the sooner the return to the habitual images. Doubtless in either case the effort is often beyond its power. Years ago I was present when a woman consulted Madame Blavatsky for a friend who saw her newly-dead husband nightly as a decaying corpse and smelt the odour of the grave. When he was dying, said Madame Blavatsky, he thought the grave the end, and now that he is dead cannot throw off that imagination. A Brahmin once told an actress friend of mine that he disliked acting, because if a man died playing Hamlet, he would be Hamlet in eternity. Yet after a time the soul partly frees itself and becomes "the shape changer" of the legends, and can cast, like the mediaeval magician, what illusions it would. There is an Irish countryman in one of Lady Gregory's books who had eaten with a stranger on the road, and some while later vomited, to discover he had but eaten chopped up grass. One thinks, too, of the spirits that show themselves in the images of wild creatures.

IX

The dead, as the passionate necessity wears out, come into a measure of freedom and may turn the impulse of events, started while living, in some new direction, but they cannot originate except through the living. Then gradually they perceive, although they are still but living in their memories, harmonies, symbols, and patterns, as though all were being refashioned by an artist, and they are moved by emotions, sweet for no imagined good but in themselves, like those of children dancing in a ring; and I do not doubt that they make love in that union which Swedenborg has said is of the whole body and seems from far off an incandescence. Hitherto shade has communicated with shade in moments of common memory that recur like the figures of a dance in terror or in joy, but now they run together like to like, and their Covens and Fleets have rhythm and pattern. This running together and running of all to a centre and yet without loss of identity, has been prepared for by their exploration of their moral life, of its beneficiaries and its victims, and even of all its untrodden paths, and all their thoughts have moulded the vehicle and become event and circumstance.

X

There are two realities, the terrestrial and the condition of fire. All power is from the terrestrial condition, for there all opposites meet and there only is the extreme of choice possible, full freedom. And there the heterogeneous is, and evil, for evil is the strain one upon another of opposites; but in the condition of fire is all music and all rest. Between is the condition of air where images have but a borrowed life, that of memory or that reflected upon them when they symbolise colours and intensities of fire, the place of shades who are "in the whirl of those who are fading," and who cry like those amorous shades in the Japanese play:

> "That we may acquire power
> Even in our faint substance,
> We will show forth even now,
> And though it be but in a dream,
> Our form of repentance."

After so many rhythmic beats the soul must cease to desire its images, and can, as it were, close its eyes.

When all sequence comes to an end, time comes to an end, and the soul puts on the rhythmic or spiritual body or luminous body and contemplates all the events of its memory and every possible impulse in an eternal possession of itself in one single moment. That condition is alone animate, all the rest is phantasy, and from thence come all the passions, and some have held, the very heat of the body.

> Time drops in decay,
> Like a candle burnt out,
> And the mountains and the woods
> Have their day, have their day.
> What one, in the rout
> Of the fire-born moods,
> Has fallen away?

XI

The soul cannot have much knowledge till it has shaken off the habit of time and of place, but till that hour it must fix its attention upon what is near, thinking of objects one after another as we run the eye or the finger over them. Its intellectual power cannot but increase and alter as its perceptions grow simultaneous. Yet even now we seem at moments to escape from time in what we call prevision, and from place when we see distant things in a dream and in concurrent dreams. A couple of years ago, while in meditation, my head seemed surrounded by a conventional sun's rays, and when I went to bed I had a long dream of a woman with her hair on fire. I awoke and lit a candle, and discovered presently from the odour that in doing so I had set my own hair on fire. I dreamed very lately that I was writing a story, and at the same time I dreamed that I was one of the characters in that story and seeking to touch the heart of some girl in defiance of the author's intention; and concurrently with all that, I was as another self trying to strike with the button of a foil a great china jar. The obscurity of the prophetic books of William Blake, which were composed in a state of vision, comes almost wholly from these concurrent dreams. Everybody has some story or some experience of the sudden knowledge in sleep or waking of some event, a misfortune for the most part happening to some friend far off.

XII

The dead living in their memories, are, I am persuaded, the source of all that we call instinct, and it is their love and their desire, all unknowing, that make us drive beyond our reason, or in defiance of our interest it may be; and it is the dream martens that, all unknowing, are master-masons to the living martens building about church windows their elaborate nests; and in their turn, the phantoms are stung to a keener delight from a concord between their luminous pure vehicle and our strong senses. It were to reproach the power or the beneficence of God, to believe those children of Alexander who died wretchedly could not throw an urnful to the heap, nor that Caesarea[2] murdered in childhood, whom Cleopatra bore to Caesar, nor that so brief- lived younger Pericles Aspasia bore being so nobly born.

XIII

Because even the most wise dead can but arrange their memories as we arrange pieces upon a chess-board and obey remembered words alone, he who would turn magician is forbidden by the Zoroastrian oracle to change "barbarous words" of invocation. Communication with *Anima Mundi* is through the association of thoughts or images or objects; and the famous dead and those of whom but a faint memory lingers, can still—and it is for no other end that, all unknowing, we value posthumous fame—tread the corridor and take the empty chair. A glove or a name can call their bearer; the shadows come to our elbow amid their old undisturbed habitations, and "materialisation" itself is easier, it may be, among walls, or by rocks and trees, that carry upon them particles the vehicles cast off in some extremity while they had still animate bodies.

Certainly the mother returns from the grave, and with arms that may be visible and solid, for a hurried moment, can comfort a neglected child or set the cradle rocking; and in all ages men have known and affirmed that when the soul is troubled, those that are a shade and a song:

> "live there,
> And live like winds of light on dark or stormy air."

XIV

Awhile they live again those passionate moments, not knowing they are dead, and then they know and may awake or half awake to be our visitors. How is their dream changed as Time drops away and their senses multiply? Does their stature alter, do their eyes grow more brilliant? Certainly the dreams stay the longer, the greater their passion when alive: Helen may still open her chamber door to Paris or watch him from the wall, and know she is dreaming but because nights and days are poignant or the stars unreckonably bright. Surely of the passionate dead we can but cry in words Ben Jonson meant for none but Shakespeare: "So rammed" are they "with life they can but grow in life with being."

XV

The inflowing from their mirrored life, who themselves receive it from the Condition of Fire, falls upon the Winding Path called the Path of the Serpent, and that inflowing coming alike to men and to animals is called natural. There is another inflow which is not natural but intellectual, and is from the fire; and it descends through souls who pass for a lengthy or a brief period out of the mirror life, as we in sleep out of the bodily life, and though it may fall upon a sleeping serpent, it falls principally upon straight paths. In so far as a man is like all other men, the inflow finds him upon the winding path, and in so far as he is a saint or sage, upon the straight path.

XVI

Daemon and man are opposites; man passes from heterogeneous objects to the simplicity of fire, and the Daemon is drawn to objects because through them he obtains power, the extremity of choice. For only in men's minds can he meet even those in the Condition of Fire who are not of his own kin. He, by using his mediatorial shades, brings man again and again to the place of choice, heightening temptation that the choice may be as final as possible, imposing his own lucidity upon events, leading his victim to whatever among works not impossible is the most difficult. He suffers with man as some firm- souled man suffers with the woman he but loves the better because she is extravagant and fickle. His descending power is neither the winding nor the straight line but zigzag, illuminating the passive and active properties, the tree's two sorts of fruit: it is the sudden lightning, for all his acts of power are instantaneous. We perceive in a pulsation of the artery, and after slowly decline.

XVII

Each Daemon is drawn to whatever man or, if its nature is more general, to whatever nation it most differs from, and it shapes into its own image the antithetical dream of man or nation. The Jews had already shown by the precious metals, by the ostentatious wealth of Solomon's temple, the passion that has made them the money-lenders of the modern world. If they had not been rapacious, lustful, narrow and persecuting beyond the people of their time, the incarnation had been impossible; but it was an intellectual impulse from the Condition of Fire that shaped their antithetical self into that of the classic world. So always it is an impulse from some Daemon that gives to our vague, unsatisfied desire, beauty, a meaning and a form all can accept.

XVIII

Only in rapid and subtle thought, or in faint accents heard in the quiet of the mind, can the thought of the spirit come to us but little changed; for a mind, that grasps objects simultaneously according to the degree of its liberation, does not think the same thought with the mind that sees objects one after another. The purpose of most religious teaching, of the insistence upon the submission to God's will above all, is to make certain of the passivity of the vehicle where it is most pure and most tenuous. When we are passive where the vehicle is coarse, we become mediumistic, and the spirits who mould themselves in that coarse vehicle can only rarely and with great difficulty speak their own thoughts and keep their own memory. They are subject to a kind of drunkenness and are stupefied, old writers said, as if with honey, and readily mistake our memory for their own, and believe themselves whom and what we please. We bewilder and overmaster them, for once they are among the perceptions of successive objects, our reason, being but an instrument created and sharpened by those objects, is stronger than their intellect, and they can but repeat with brief glimpses from another state, our knowledge and our words.

XIX

A friend once dreamed that she saw many dragons climbing upon the steep side of a cliff and continually falling. Henry More thought that those who, after centuries of life, failed to find the rhythmic body and to pass into the Condition of Fire, were born again. Edmund Spenser, who was among More's masters, affirmed that nativity without giving it a cause:

> "After that they againe retourned beene,
> They in that garden planted be agayne,
> And grow afresh, as they had never seene
> Fleshy corruption, nor mortal payne.
> Some thousand years so doen they ther remayne,
> And then of him are clad with other hew,
> Or sent into the chaungeful world agayne,

Till thither they retourn where first they grew:
So like a wheele, around they roam from old to new."

The dead who speak to us deny metempsychosis, perhaps because they but know a little better what they knew alive; while the dead in Asia, for perhaps no better reason, affirm it, and so we are left amid plausibilities and uncertainties.

XX

But certainly it is always to the Condition of Fire, where emotion is not brought to any sudden stop, where there is neither wall nor gate, that we would rise; and the mask plucked from the oak-tree is but my imagination of rhythmic body. We may pray to that last condition by any name so long as we do not pray to it as a thing or a thought, and most prayers call it man or woman or child:

"For mercy has a human heart,
Pity a human face."

Within ourselves Reason and Will, who are the man and woman, hold out towards a hidden altar, a laughing or crying child.

XXI

When I remember that Shelley calls our minds "mirrors of the fire for which all thirst," I cannot but ask the question all have asked, "What or who has cracked the mirror?" I begin to study the only self that I can know, myself, and to wind the thread upon the perne again.

At certain moments, always unforeseen, I become happy, most commonly when at hazard I have opened some book of verse. Sometimes it is my own verse when, instead of discovering new technical flaws, I read with all the excitement of the first writing. Perhaps I am sitting in some crowded restaurant, the open book beside me, or closed, my excitement having over-brimmed the page. I look at the strangers near as if I had known them all my life, and it seems strange that I cannot speak to them: everything fills me with affection, I have no longer any fears or any needs; I do not even remember that this happy mood must come to an end. It seems as if the vehicle had suddenly grown pure and far extended and so luminous that one half imagines that the images from *Anima Mundi*, embodied there and drunk with that sweetness, would, as some country drunkard who had thrown a wisp into his own thatch, burn up time.

It may be an hour before the mood passes, but latterly I seem to understand that I enter upon it the moment I cease to hate. I think the common condition of our life is hatred—I know that this is so with me—irritation with public or private events or persons. There is no great matter in forgetfulness of servants, or the delays of tradesmen, but how forgive the ill-breeding of Carlyle, or the rhetoric of Swinburne, or that woman who murmurs over the dinner-table the opinion of her daily paper? And only a week ago last Sunday, I hated the spaniel who disturbed a partridge on her nest, a trout who took my bait and yet broke away unhooked. The books say that our happiness comes from the opposite of hate, but I am not certain, for we may love unhappily. And plainly, when I have closed a book too stirred to go on reading, and in those brief intense visions of sleep, I have something about me that, though it makes me love, is more like innocence. I am in the place where the daemon is, but I do not think he is with me until I begin to make a new personality, selecting among those images, seeking always to satisfy a hunger grown out of conceit with daily diet; and yet as I write the words, "I select," I am full of uncertainty, not knowing when I am the finger, when the clay. Once, twenty years ago, I seemed to awake from sleep to find my body rigid, and to hear a strange voice speaking these words through my lips as through lips of stone: "We make an image of him who sleeps, and it is not him who sleeps, and we call it Emmanuel."

XXII

As I go up and down my stair and pass the gilded Moorish wedding-chest where I keep my "barbarous words," I wonder will I take to them once more, for I am baffled by those voices that still speak as to Odysseus but as the bats; or now that I shall in a little be growing old, to some kind of simple piety like that of an old woman.

May 9, 1917.

EPILOGUE

M<small>Y</small> D<small>EAR</small> "M<small>AURICE</small>"—I was often in France before you were born or when you were but a little child. When I went for the first or second time Mallarmé had just written: "All our age is full of the trembling of the veil of the temple." One met everywhere young men of letters who talked of magic. A distinguished English man of letters asked me to call with him on Stanislas de Gaeta because he did not dare go alone to that mysterious house. I met from time to time with the German poet Doukenday, a grave Swede whom I only discovered after years to have been Strindberg, then looking for the philosopher's stone in a lodging near the Luxembourg; and one day in the chambers of Stuart Merrill the poet, I spoke with a young Arabic scholar who displayed a large, roughly-made gold ring which had grown to the shape of his finger. Its gold had no hardening alloy, he said, because it was made by his master, a Jewish Rabbi, of alchemical gold. My critical mind—was it friend or enemy?—mocked, and yet I was delighted. Paris was as legendary as Connaught. This new pride, that of the adept, was added to the pride of the artist. Villiers de L'Isle Adam, the haughtiest of men, had but lately died. I had read his *Axel* slowly and laboriously as one reads a sacred book—my French was very bad—and had applauded it upon the stage. As I could not follow the spoken words, I was not bored even where Axel and the Commander discussed philosophy for a half-hour instead of beginning their duel. If I felt impatient it was only that they delayed the coming of the adept Janus, for I hoped to recognise the moment when Axel cries: "I know that lamp, it was burning before Solomon"; or that other when he cries: "As for living, our servants will do that for us."

The movement of letters had been haughty even before Magic had touched it. Rimbaud had sung: "Am I an old maid that I should fear the embrace of death?" And everywhere in Paris and in London young men boasted of the garret, and claimed to have no need of what the crowd values.

Last summer you, who were at the age I was when first I heard of Mallarmé and of Verlaine, spoke much of the French poets young men and women read to-day. Claudel I already somewhat knew, but you read to me for the first time from Jammes a dialogue between a poet and a bird, that made us cry, and a whole volume of Peguy's *Mystère de la Charité de Jeanne d'Arc*. Nothing remained the same but the preoccupation with religion, for these poets submitted everything to the Pope, and all, even Claudel, a proud oratorical man, affirmed that they saw the world with the eyes of vine-dressers and charcoal-burners. It was no longer the soul, self-moving and self-teaching—

the magical soul—but Mother France and Mother Church.

Have not my thoughts run through a like round, though I have not found my tradition in the Catholic Church, which was not the church of my childhood, but where the tradition is, as I believe, more universal and more ancient?

W. B. Y.

May 11, 1917.